Published by Ladybird Books Ltd
80 Strand, London WC2R ORL

A Penguin Company

www.ladybird.co.uk

Printed in Italy

Disney's

The Jungle Book 2

Ladybird

Mowgli liked living in the man-village, but it was different from the jungle. Here, there were always rules to obey.

Mowgli lived with Ranjan and his family now. His best friend was a girl called Shanti. She and Ranjan loved to hear stories about Mowgli's jungle adventures.

Even though they knew Shanti was afraid of the jungle, Mowgli and Ranjan still played tricks on her. She went for water one day and Mowgli warned, "Yesterday, I saw tiger tracks here." Ranjan let out a ROAR! from the bushes and Shanti screamed in terror.

Annoyed, Shanti swept off. "Why are you scared of the jungle?" Ranjan asked.

"Because it's dangerous," snapped Shanti.

Soon Mowgli wandered over and, trying to impress, picked a banana and squeezed the delicious fruit straight into Ranjan's mouth! "Just a trick I learned in the jungle," he grinned.

Now it was Shanti's turn. She threw a mango into the air, and it peeled itself on a branch as it fell into her hand. "A little trick I learned right here at home," she said breezily.

"Oh, don't listen to us, Ranjan!" laughed Mowgli. "Listen to the jungle. When you hear that rhythm, you get a crazy feeling inside!" He danced, and soon Shanti and all the village children were following him.

Suddenly Shanti yelled, "Stop!" They were almost in the jungle!

Ranjan's father heard Shanti's cry and came running. "Come inside!" he scolded. "The jungle is a dangerous place!"

Mowgli got into trouble for putting the children in danger.

That night he gazed sadly at the distant jungle. He missed his life there – but most of all he missed his old friend Baloo.

Meanwhile, deep in the jungle, Bagheera the panther was worried. He knew Baloo was missing Mowgli too, and wanted his playmate back. He watched as Baloo wandered towards the man-village to look for Mowgli. He caught up with him at the river.

"Mowgli must stay in the village with his own kind," said Bagheera, sternly.

"Out of the way, Baggy," said Baloo, sadly.

Bagheera asked Colonel Hathi and his elephants to help. They stood firm, blocking the path. Baloo knew what to do and dived into the river! When he came up for air at the river bank, only Baby Elephant could see him. "This way. Quick!" he whispered, and showed Baloo another route to the village.

The villagers were asleep when Baloo got there. Under the twinkling stars, he looked for Mowgli. But someone else was prowling around. It was Shere Khan. He was looking for the man-cub, too. He wanted to kill him.

Baloo went from hut to hut until he found what he was looking for. "Papa Bear! Am I glad to see you!" smiled Mowgli. They spoke in whispers, happy to be together.

Shanti was wandering in the village, too.
She came round a corner to see Mowgli
being tossed around by a huge bear!

"Help!" she screamed. "Wild animal!"

"Where?" cried Baloo, frightened.
Grabbing Mowgli, he ran for the jungle.

Shanti's scream brought the villagers running. But instead of seeing Baloo, they came face to face with Shere Khan, the most evil tiger of them all. Bravely, they drove the growling tiger back to the jungle.

Shanti hadn't seen Shere Khan. She was running the other way, after Baloo. "Wait for me!" cried Ranjan, following her.

Soon she and Ranjan realised they were lost. "Mowgli's in trouble and we're going to find him!" Ranjan said, bravely.

Shere Kahn was searching, too. "Where's Mowgli?" he growled at Kaa the snake, a paw round his skinny neck.

"At the ssswamp," lied Kaa, desperate to escape.

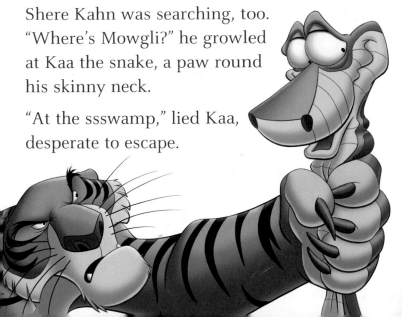

Bagheera, meanwhile, was on jungle patrol when he found himself in the middle of an elephant stampede. "What's happening?" he cried, trying not to be trampled.

"Man is in the jungle," they chorused.

Bagheera realised what had happened. Mowgli was in the jungle, with Baloo.

In another part of the jungle, Baloo was eating a mango peeled for him by Mowgli.

"Where'd you learn that?" he asked.

"Shanti showed me," said Mowgli.

Suddenly Baloo pushed Mowgli out of sight. Bagheera was coming. "The villagers are searching for Mowgli," said the panther, patiently; "Have you seen him?"

"Sorry, Baggy. Wish I could help," lied Baloo.

Bagheera wandered off, leaving Baloo and Mowgli alone. "We can't let anybody see you," said Baloo, looking around, nervously.

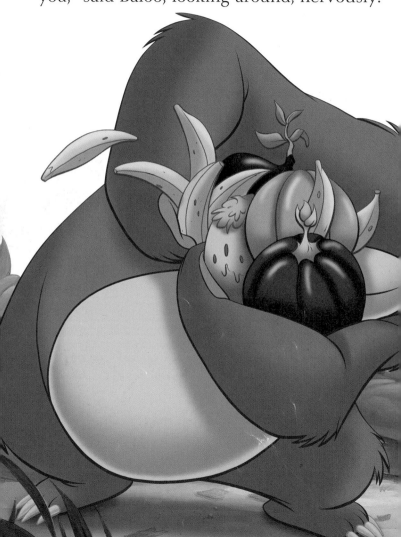

"Wow! The villagers must really miss me if they've come into the jungle," said Mowgli, surprised. "I wonder if Shanti's with them?"

"You don't want *her* to find you! What will you do if she does?" asked Baloo, worried.

"You're going to have to scare her!" said Mowgli to the gentle bear.

Baloo took a deep breath and then let out an enormous ROAR!

Shanti and Ranjan trudged along. As Shanti tried to work out where they were, Ranjan found some mango peel. "Mowgli must have been here!" cried Shanti.

By now, Shere Khan had reached the swamp, with no sign of Mowgli. He had been tricked. "He's headed downriver with a bear," said Lucky, a meddlesome vulture.

Baloo took Mowgli to his hideout. There was a baboon band playing! "They don't swing like this in your village, do they, kid?" teased Baloo. Mowgli didn't like them making fun of the village, and wandered off by himself.

After walking for miles, Shanti heard singing. It was Mowgli! "We came to save you from that wild bear," she explained.

Baloo had come looking for Mowgli, too. He saw Shanti and charged. Shanti thought he was a wild bear, until he got a little tangled up in some vines. But then he let out a roar, and brave Shanti bopped him on the nose!

Mowgli tried to explain who Baloo was, but it all came out wrong. Shanti stomped off, taking Ranjan with her.

When Mowgli caught up with them, Shanti was standing, frozen to the spot in terror. Shere Khan was staring calmly at them, licking his lips.

"Run!" whispered Mowgli.

Mowgli led Shere Khan to some ruins,
Shanti and Ranjan close behind. Baloo
found Ranjan just when he was struggling
to keep up and handed him to Bagheera
to look after. He caught up with Shanti.
"I'm here to help Mowgli," they both
said together, and ran on, friends at last.

They found Mowgli and between them
kept Shere Khan at bay. But Mowgli and
Shanti knew they were at his mercy.

"So, who's it going to be man-cub? You or your girlfriend," Shere Khan smiled cruelly. "I'm waiting. One . . . two . . ."

"No, don't!" cried Mowgli.

Suddenly, the massive tiger sprang. Mowgli and Shanti ran for their lives as Shere Khan chased them up the face of an ancient stone tiger. Suddenly, before their eyes, it cracked and the huge stone head toppled and fell onto Shere Khan. He was trapped. They were safe at last.

Later, Mowgli watched as Shanti and
Ranjan went to meet the villagers. "I belong
with them," he said, sadly. "But I'm going
to miss you, Papa Bear."

"Me too, Little Britches," sighed Baloo.

They hugged, then Mowgli walked slowly
towards his friends, and his family.

The villagers scooped the three children up joyfully, and headed home.

Life in the man-village was soon back to normal, almost. Now, whenever they fetched water, Mowgli, Shanti and Ranjan crossed the river to do a little singing and a little boogie woogie with their friends, Baloo and Bagheera. Mowgli was truly happy. All his friends and family were together at last.